THE *FANTASTIC* BOOK OF
In-line SKATING

ALDIE CHALMERS

COPPER BEECH BOOKS
BROOKFIELD, CONNECTICUT

*Designed and
produced by*
Aladdin Books Ltd
28 Percy Street
London W1P 0LD

*First published in
the United States in 1997 by*
Copper Beech Books,
an imprint of
The Millbrook Press
2 Old New Milford Road
Brookfield, Connecticut 06804

Editor
Sarah Levete
Design
David West Children's
Book Design
Designer
Flick Killerby
Illustrator
Catherine Ward
Picture Research
Brooks Krikler Research

Printed in Belgium
All rights reserved
5 4 3 2 1

**Library of Congress
Cataloging-in-Publication Data**
Chalmers, Aldie.
In-line skating / by Aldie Chalmers ;
illustrated by Catherine Ward.
p. cm. — (The fantastic book of—)
Includes index.
Summary: Discusses the history and
techniques of and safety measures for
in-line skating, with fold-out pages
on skating events.
ISBN 0-7613-0623-4 (lib. bdg.).
ISBN 0-7613-0638-2 (trade hardcover)
1. In-line skating—Juvenile literature.
[1. In-line skating.] I. Ward, Catherine,
ill. II. Title. III. Series.
GV859.73.C53 1997   97-10590
796.21—dc21   CIP AC

CONTENTS

Introduction

In-line skating is one of the world's fastest growing sports. Join the millions of people, of every age and type, who enjoy the exercise and exhilaration of in-line skating.

Today's in-line skates are made with the most up-to-date high-tech materials available. Roller skates, or "quads," have been transformed from bulky skates with wheels arranged in a rectangle into compact, light, streamlined skates, with the wheels arranged in a straight line.

Whether or not you are an experienced skater, this book tells you everything you need to know about in-line skating from care of your skates to styling big airs, or jumps. When you are confident with the basic steps to get you moving, try some more advanced moves and tricks. But whatever your level, only try new moves when you are confident and sure that you can safely practice them.

An eight-page fold-out goes behind the scenes at an extreme or, as it is more usually known, "aggressive" competition. "Aggressive" skating is not, as its name suggests, to do with aggression – rather it takes the sport to its limits, using props such as rails and ramps *(right)*.

In-line skating is fun but it is also a demanding sport. Every skater should wear full protective clothing to stay safe and to get the most from in-line skating.

Read this book – put on your pads, helmet, and skates – and get rolling!

4

Taking up in-line skating

Today, in-line skating is a serious sport for professional in-line skaters as well as an extremely popular recreational activity. There are several types of in-line skating – the skates and equipment for each type have become very specialized.

If you are taking up the sport for the first time, begin as a general or "recreational" skater, or "rec" for short. You can then decide if you want to try another style of skating – "aggressive", freestyle, hockey, or speed skating. Whichever form of in-line skating you take up, you are guaranteed to have fun.

SOME REASONS TO START IN-LINE SKATING...
If you are in any doubt about why in-line skating is so popular, then read on. Readers of an international skating magazine wrote in saying why they began in-line skating.

There's all the fun of skiing but no need for snow; all the fun of ice skating without the need for ice... All you need is your skates, your protective gear, and some space... I'm addicted to the buzz... It's for girls and boys... It's for all ages... I live on my skates, they never leave my feet... It's exhilarating... It's the best sport I've ever tried... There's so many ways to use your skates – "aggressive," hockey, speed, recreation, and fitness, or just as a cool form of transportation... It's a great way to get to school... It's brilliant to skate with friends... The whole family can do it... You can just do it for fun or take it all the way to the world championships!

"REC" AND FREESTYLE
"Rec" skating forms the largest group of all skaters. It's about having fun and enjoying the thrill of free-wheeling. The most advanced form of "rec" is freestyle – new moves and tricks, often performed to dance music.

RACES FOR FUN
Everyone can enjoy skating just for fun or at a more competitive level.

Why not join in a "rat race?" You pay a small registration fee to enter a race with other people your age. Both in-line and quad skaters are racing to the finish line in a rat race (left).

BEGIN AT THE BEGINNING

To begin with, all you need is a pair of in-line skates, the protective clothing, and an empty space. But in-line skates and the necessary equipment can be expensive. If you have not previously tried in-line skating, you can rent the skates and equipment before buying them.

Many beginners also benefit from having some lessons with a qualified in-line skating instructor. This can prevent you from picking up any bad skating habits. In-line skating magazines will have the latest news of competitions, moves, and in-line skating associations. Contact your national association for the names and addresses of recommended instructors.

SKATING FOR EVERYONE

Enjoy your skating with a group of others *(above)* or on your own. Hockey, on in-line skates or quads *(left),* is a great team sport. Why not form a team with your friends and enter a league? Or join a speed-skating club where you can compete and train with others – and have a good time. "Aggressive" skaters often form a "posse" or "crew" to practice, or "session," and compete together *(right).*

To take your skating to a more serious level, begin with local league competitions and progress to national and international competitions. There are currently world championship events for in-line speed and "aggressive" skating and in-line hockey.

7

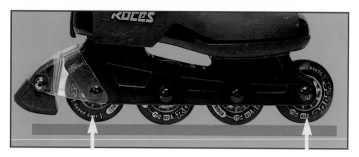

"Rockered" system

"Anti-rockered" system

ROCKING AND ROLLING

On most skates you can adjust the height of your wheels to create different skating effects. Lower the two center wheels to create a "rockering" effect which allows you to turn more effectively.

With all the wheels flat, you can turn less easily, but you gain more speed. Raise the two middle wheels or replace them with smaller wheels for "anti-rockering." "Aggressive" skaters use this to "lock on" better to rails when grinding *(see pages 18 and 23).*

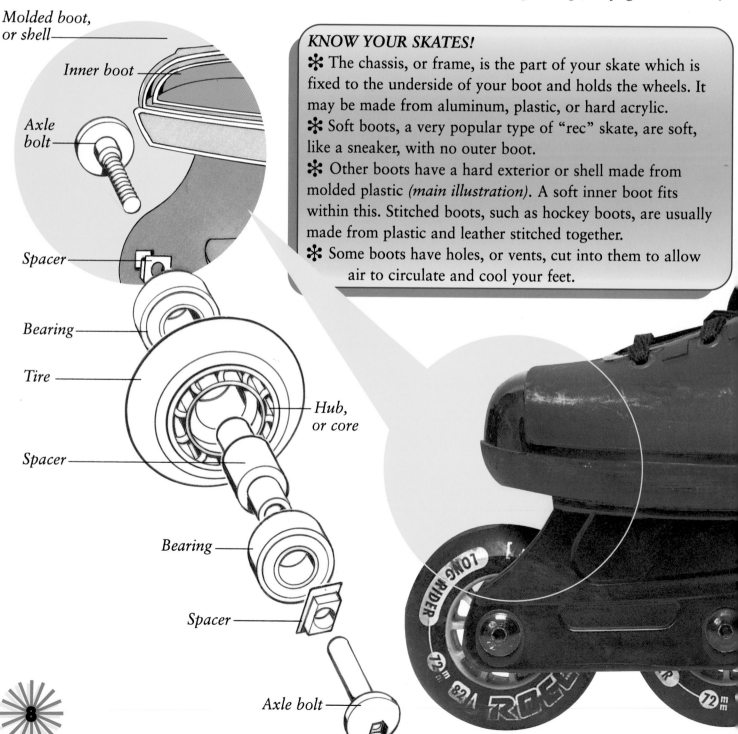

Molded boot, or shell

Inner boot

Axle bolt

Spacer

Bearing

Tire

Spacer

Hub, or core

Bearing

Spacer

Axle bolt

KNOW YOUR SKATES!

✳ The chassis, or frame, is the part of your skate which is fixed to the underside of your boot and holds the wheels. It may be made from aluminum, plastic, or hard acrylic.

✳ Soft boots, a very popular type of "rec" skate, are soft, like a sneaker, with no outer boot.

✳ Other boots have a hard exterior or shell made from molded plastic *(main illustration)*. A soft inner boot fits within this. Stitched boots, such as hockey boots, are usually made from plastic and leather stitched together.

✳ Some boots have holes, or vents, cut into them to allow air to circulate and cool your feet.

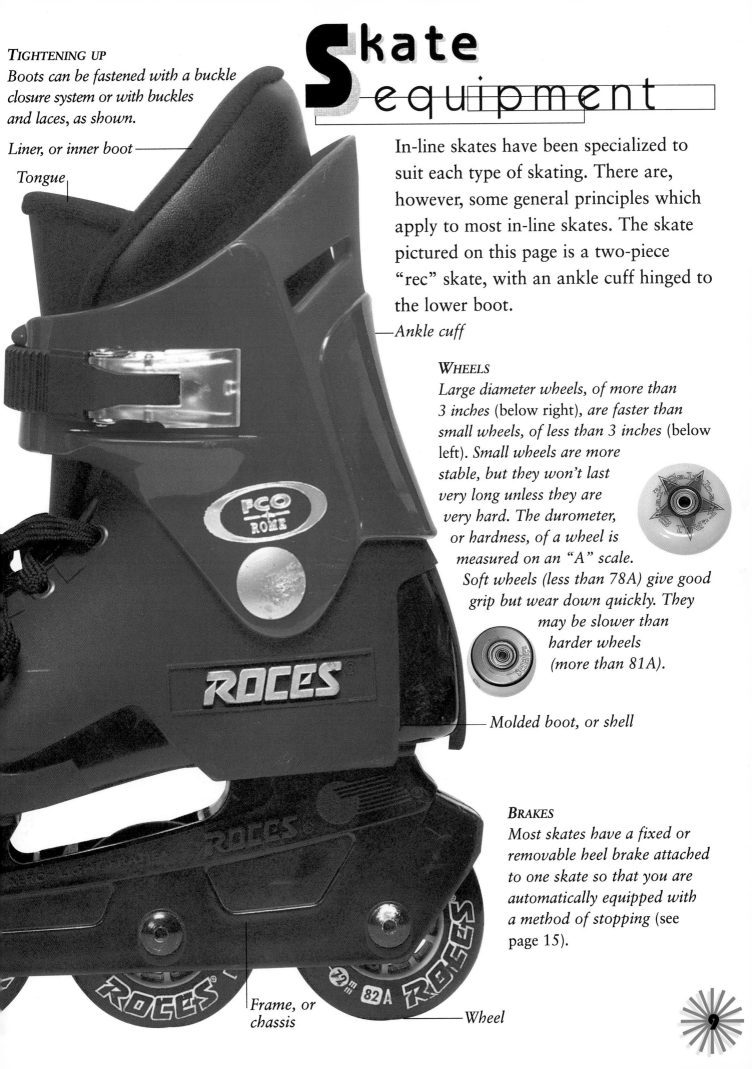

TIGHTENING UP
Boots can be fastened with a buckle closure system or with buckles and laces, as shown.

Liner, or inner boot ————

Tongue

In-line skates have been specialized to suit each type of skating. There are, however, some general principles which apply to most in-line skates. The skate pictured on this page is a two-piece "rec" skate, with an ankle cuff hinged to the lower boot.

—Ankle cuff

WHEELS
Large diameter wheels, of more than 3 inches (below right), are faster than small wheels, of less than 3 inches (below left). Small wheels are more stable, but they won't last very long unless they are very hard. The durometer, or hardness, of a wheel is measured on an "A" scale. Soft wheels (less than 78A) give good grip but wear down quickly. They may be slower than harder wheels (more than 81A).

—— Molded boot, or shell

BRAKES
Most skates have a fixed or removable heel brake attached to one skate so that you are automatically equipped with a method of stopping (see page 15).

Frame, or chassis

—— Wheel

9

Skate gear for safety

Skating on hard surfaces can do a lot of damage to your elbows, knees, and your head if you fall. It is important to pad up before you even put your skates on. Try to get the best protective clothing that you can afford – the better the equipment, the more it will protect you. Wearing pads actually helps you to skate better because it gives you the confidence to fall safely. Remember, if you fall you want to scrape the plastic of your pads, NOT your soft flesh.

SHORTS

A bit of extra padding can make all the difference if you fall! Wear pants or baggy shorts that are fitted with extra padding (below) for your hips and your backside. If you wear sweatpants or leggings, sew in some thick foam to create extra padding.

SAVE YOUR HEAD

You can buy specialized in-line skating helmets (above) from most skate shops. Make sure that the helmet is the right size for your head, and wear it – it's your only head!

LOOKS GOOD

Elbows are very vulnerable and must be protected with elbow pads (above). Wrist guards (right) look cool – and they protect your wrists and hands.

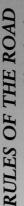

KNEES

If you fall, you should fall forward onto your knees (see page 13). Protect your knees with well-fitting knee pads (below).

RULES OF THE ROAD

Look after yourself and others when you are out skating:

✱ Always wear the correct protective clothing and make sure you have lights and reflective strips for skating in the dark.

✱ Make sure your equipment is in good working order.

✱ Always tell an adult where you are going to be skating and at what time you will be back.

✱ Only skate in areas where it is allowed. Avoid traffic. Where permission is given to skate in parking lot, make sure it is not in use.

✱ Show consideration to pedestrians.

✱ Observe all the traffic regulations. If you don't, you put yourself and others at great risk.

SAFETY

Safety doesn't just mean protective clothing. It means following the rules of the road (*below right*). If you think you may be skating when it gets dark, take a light with you. Attach a light to the back of your helmet – check the batteries before you set out. Buy lights that clip onto your boots (*left*), or attach regular bike lights with some stick-on Velcro strips. Wear a reflective band or strip across your body – the brighter the better!

CHOOSE CAREFULLY!

Make sure that you use skates that are appropriate to the style of your in-line skating. You will be very uncomfortable if your boots don't fit, so make sure you get the right size. Your foot should feel secure but not restricted within your boot – you should be able to wiggle your toes. Spend as much time as you need when you buy or rent a pair of skates – otherwise you will be uncomfortable, and your skating will suffer.

STRETCH YOUR CHEST
Interlock your hands behind your body. Extend your arms behind you and raise them upward slightly.

STRETCH YOUR UPPER BACK
Interlock your hands and stretch your arms out in front of you. Repeat the exercise, but with your palms turned away from your body.

STRETCH YOUR UPPER THIGHS
Stand on one leg with your knee slightly bent. Bend your other leg back. Hold your ankle with your hand. Keeping your knees together, pull your raised leg toward your backside. Push your foot against your hand.

STRETCH THE BACK OF YOUR THIGHS
Extend one leg forward. Bend the other leg slightly, placing your hands lightly on your upper thigh. Bring your weight over your extended leg.

STRETCH YOUR HIPS
Extend one leg backward and place your knee on the floor. Bend your other leg in front of you. Bring your weight slightly forward, keeping the knee of your front leg at a right angle to your foot.

STRETCH YOUR INNER THIGHS
Sit upright with your legs apart and your hands in front of your body. Gently press forward, keeping your legs extended.

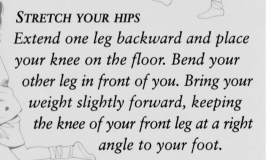

WARM UP AND STRETCH

Stretching *(left)* reduces the chance of injury or strain to your body. It also increases your flexibility (the range of movement in your body) and improves your performance. It is important to warm up gradually. Always stretch slowly and never bounce in a stretch. And don't forget to stretch both legs!

Getting started

You've got the skates, you've got the gear – now get going – on your stretches! Skating is a physical activity so you should always warm up and stretch before doing it.

When you first start skating, your skates will feel very strange. Practice the technique for getting up safely. Once you are up, make sure you always adopt a good "ready position." You will inevitably fall over at some point in your skating career – so learn how to fall safely.

1

GETTING UP

Get up the easy and safe way! Bend down on your hands and knees, with the toes of your skates touching the ground 1. Bring one leg forward (keeping it bent) so that the wheels of the skate are in contact with the ground.

LEARNING HOW TO FALL

You should try to fall the shortest distance possible, which is forward onto your knee pads. If your knees are bent before the fall, the impact or force with which you hit the ground is greatly reduced. When you fall forward try to protect your head and face. The best position is on your elbow pads with your hands outstretched in front of you *(below left)*.

Try to avoid falling backward – because you'll have farther to fall. However, if you do fall backward, don't try to get your hands under your body to break the fall because you may well injure your wrists. Instead, try to twist at the waist so that the top half of your body is facing the direction of the fall *(right)*. But, as you already know, falling safely can only be safe if you are wearing the correct protective clothing.

When you first practice getting up, hold on to a stable post or bar with one hand.

2

3

4

Place both your hands on your raised knee ☐2. Support your weight with your hands on your raised knee. As you straighten the raised leg, you will come to a standing position ☐3. Keep your legs slightly bent and your weight slightly forward ☐4. This is your basic ready position.

In position
When you first wear skates, you may want to stand upright. However, the ready position (knees bent and weight slightly forward) will help you keep your balance and stop you falling backward. Very skilled skaters, who may skate with their knees straight, adopt the ready position just before stopping, or when they wish to become more stable.

In the ready position bring your feet to a "V" shape. Point both skates outward 1 .

Raise your right skate slightly and place it in front of you. Your weight is on your left trailing skate 2 .

Direction of travel

Moving forward

Don't just pad up, aim yourself down the road, and go – that's the best way to have a nasty accident. Start with the "duck" walk on grass or on a thick carpet.

When you become used to the feel of this, practice striding on your skates. This is like the "duck" walk but, instead of lifting up your skates, you use a stroking and gliding movement. When you move forward you steer with your front, or leading, skate – it is positioned in the direction in which you are traveling. You push and thrust with your back, or trailing, skate. Remember, if you lean backward you will stop moving forward – but you will start to fall backward!

Bring your left skate through the "V" position 3 *; place it in front of you* 4 *. Repeat steps 1-4. This is the "duck" walk.*

14

First practice on grass.

STROKING AND GLIDING

From the "V" position, thrust back and slightly out to the side with the trailing skate. As you do so, momentarily transfer your weight from the front skate to the trailing skate, shown by the blue triangle *(left)*. This stroke powers forward movement. Transfer your weight to the front skate as you glide, or coast, on this skate. Bring your trailing foot to the front to continue the sequence. The stroking and gliding action is called striding.

To stroke (see right), thrust with your weight from your trailing skate.

HEEL-BRAKE STOP

Find a smooth, level area, free of obstacles such as twigs or cracks in the pavement. Scissor your legs so that your skate with the heel brake is in the front position. Point the toe of this skate upward; your heel brake comes in contact with the ground. Don't try to stop right away – bring the brake into contact with the ground very lightly at first. Slowly add more pressure to the heel brake. Concentrate on keeping your balance.

A-FRAME TURN

This is a simple way to turn (above). Roll forward slowly, taking your skates to a wide stance. Your skates point forward. To turn to the right, shift your weight onto your left skate. Without lifting your skates off the ground, apply slight pressure to your left skate so that the heel is being pushed outward and the toe is being pushed inward. This will start the turn. Keep your weight and pressure on the left skate to complete the turn. Do not stroke during the turn.

RACE EVENTS
In many countries, speed skating associations organize competitions and events for all age groups and abilities. Start with a fun race (see page 7). If you enjoy it, why not join a speed club and start entering races (left)?

RACING TO THE TOP
Sutton (Sooty) Atkins, shown in the lead (*above left*), is one of Britain's top speed skaters. When he discovered the thrill of the sport he began a local speed club. He now travels the world to train, compete, and coach.

Speed skating

One of the most exciting areas of in-line skating is speed skating, a fast and demanding sport. Speed skaters can reach speeds of up to 26 miles per hour. Race distances vary from short sprints of an eighth of a mile to endurance races of 62 miles. You can compete in races at a local club level – and if you have the skill you may even reach the World Championships.

To reduce wind resistance and therefore to increase their speed, some speed skaters may wear a Lycra cover over their skates (right).

TECHNIQUE
A speed skater must keep his or her body lower to the ground than that of a "rec" in-liner. By being low (as shown in the illustrations), your skates are in contact with the ground for longer and you will achieve a longer push and thrust. Speed skates are very light and strong and they are specially molded to fit the skater's foot exactly! Most speed skates have a five-wheel frame that is faster than the four-wheel "rec" skate.

RACING GEAR
In races speed skaters wear helmets similar to cycle helmets and streamlined Lycra "skin suits." Elbow, knee, or wrist protection is not worn because these would slow down the skaters. However, all races are strictly supervised to make them as safe as possible.

Aggressive Skating

"Aggressive" skating is not about rolling along smooth, flat surfaces with all your wheels in contact with the ground – it's about launching into the air and grinding your skates along different surfaces. In competition, "aggressive" skating is divided into ramp and street skating. To succeed you need lots of imagination and creativity as well as daring and skill.

RAMP SKATING

This developed on the ramps originally built for skateboarding and BMX-biking. Ramps allow "aggressive" skaters to show off their style and to develop their technique. They vary from the huge "vert" ramp (right) *which is a half pipe more than 10 feet high, to the smaller mini half-pipe ramp and different-sized quarter-pipe ramps* (see page 21).

STREET SKATING

Street skating first began on city streets. It is made up of big airs and stylish grinds (below). *Tricks and moves are performed on an amazing variety of surfaces, including a "fun box" with ramps and rails* (above).

"AGGRESSIVE" SKATE SPEAK

✳ *Air – jump*
✳ *Grommet – a very young aggressive skater*
✳ *Lid – a helmet*
✳ *Pavement inspector – a beginner*
✳ *Phat or rad – a good, stylish move*
✳ *Sessioning or jamming – spending time skating in an area or on a particular rail or ramp*
✳ *Slam – falling or crashing*

INSPIRATION
Music blaring, crowds cheering – in competition, these can inspire and encourage the successful "aggressive" skater.

NEW MOVES

The Aggressive Skating Association which organizes major championships also monitors judging to ensure that it is consistent worldwide. Judges *(above)* are themselves "aggressive" skaters so they will know how to judge the latest moves that skaters develop. Different skaters often call the same move by a different name.

THE CROWD

The enthusiastic crowd, both inside the competition course (above) and in the surrounding area, makes the atmosphere electric. Video shows, torch-light processions, fun events, and promotional giveaways by in-line skating manufacturers add to the buzz for everyone from skater to spectator.

Grinding

Grinding is a major part of "aggressive" skating. It is extremely popular, but it requires great skill and balance to execute these moves. It is essential that you wear the full protective clothing at all times.

Grinding is most often done on curbs, rails *(left)*, concrete ledges, or other hard surfaces that a skater can "lock" onto.

You can begin at any age.

To match the skill and imagination behind the performance of grinds, "aggressive" skaters invent personalized names for the moves, such as the "fishbrain," (right), shown by Jon Julio. (See page 23 for more grinds).

Everybody's watching!

THE GRIND

With a grind plate attached to the chassis of each of your aggressive skates *(see page 19)*, grinds are performed by balancing while sliding along a part of your skate other than your wheels. To "lock on" to a prop such as a rail, you can use the sole of your boot, the side of the chassis, the part of the chassis exposed by the gap between your wheels, and even the top of the skates where the laces are!

Watching the professionals!

The Extreme Event

The COMPETITION

In-liners from around the world will gather for a major international "aggressive"

skating competition or event which may be held over three days. While the skaters are practicing grinds and jumps, the arena is set up. A master of ceremonies (MC) starts things off *(left)*. Most "aggressive" competitions feature two main contests – street and ramp. Some will also feature high jump competitions, downhill races, and road races.

THE PARTICIPANTS
Most skaters save hard to be at an event. A lucky few competitors may have sponsorship.

A *"backslide"*
grind (left)

A *"unity"*
grind
(right)

STREET

A street course may consist of quarter pipes, ramps, handrails, and fun boxes. A course in a competition at Lausanne, Switzerland, in 1996 included a police car with grind rails welded to the hood and to the roof! Of course grinds (*see pages 18 and 23*) are also a key feature of street skating (*above and left*). "Aggressive" skates (*right*) are built to resist the challenges of the sport.

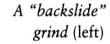

"Aggressive" skate

STYLE IS ALL
*The best skater makes every
move look effortless and smooth,
such as the well-styled "crossed
rocket" (left).*

An air from a quarter pipe (above).

RAMPS

Most competitions include several
ramps of different sizes. A half pipe ramp is made up of a platform, or
deck, up to 10 feet high, and a curved area called the transition. A "vert"
ramp includes a vertical section, usually 6 inches – but it can be as high as
2 feet. On the "vert" ramp, judges will be impressed by the skater reaching
heights above the coping (the point where the "vert" meets the deck).
Styled spins, airs *(below)*, and lip tricks *(see pages 22 and 23)* will all
earn the competitor points.

VARIATION
*The mark of an exceptional
skater is the ability to devise
variations on different moves
– and to do so with style
(right). To make the winning run,
a skater has to combine creativity,
skill, and a radical approach.
"Tweaking" or exaggerating tricks
and moves will add to the
skater's score.*

Skate Parks

At all levels, "aggressive skaters" need to practice and develop new moves. With good equipment, including specially made ramps, skate parks are ideal for this. If you are new to "aggressive" skating, a skate park is the best and safest place to begin. You will be able to watch experienced skaters try out the latest moves. Competitions are often held in skate parks – if you don't feel ready to enter as a competitor, it's great fun to watch *(right)*.

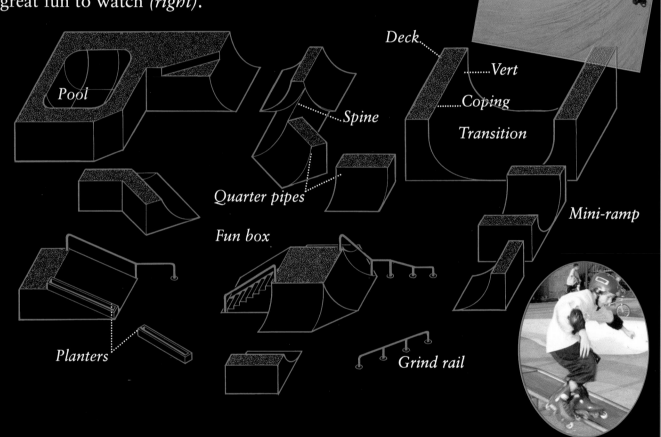

Pool

Deck

Vert

Coping

Transition

Spine

Quarter pipes

Mini-ramp

Fun box

Planters

Grind rail

PERKS OF A PARK

Learn new tricks, meet other skaters, and have hours of fun in a skate park. A good skate park will have a variety of ramps and equipment, from hand-rails to planters (concrete or metal blocks), to re-create a "street" scene.

SKATE IN SAFETY
Most parks are designed with safety in mind, but you will need to wear your full safety equipment (above).

SPINS AND CABS

For extra points, skaters add spins, or "cabs," to their tricks. Every launch should be styled. For instance, a move may be "mute" – with your knees pulled up to your chest and your arm reaching across your legs and body to grab the outside edge of your opposite skate. Or it may be "stale" – reaching down with one arm behind your legs and thigh to grab the heel of your opposite skate. Rotations of 180° *(above)* or 360° *(right)* are an added feature.

`IT'S ALL UPSIDE DOWN!
The "hand plant" or "invert" is performed on the coping as a lip trick (right).

SLAMMING
Even the best skater will occasionally "slam", or fall. This is why it is essential to wear the correct protective clothing *(above)*.

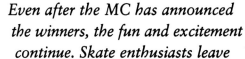

LOOKING TO THE FUTURE
Even after the MC has announced the winners, the fun and excitement continue. Skate enthusiasts leave the competition inspired by new moves, and eager to try them out – in preparation for the next event.

More Grinding

New grinds and tricks are being invented all the time. The photographs *(right)* show some common grinds. Each move can be performed "unnatural." This means that a skater approaches a rail from his or her left side even though it would feel more natural to approach it from his or her right side.

"Criste grind"

"Rocket makio"

"Backslide"

"Acid muso"

"Backslide"

"Soul grind"

"Royale"

If you prefer speed, try downhill racing, often included at an "aggressive" event.

The emphasis is on fun.

Racing can have its downside too!

TOP SCORER

Judges mark competitors using a point system. They look for style, difficulty and technique, and consistency of landings and line – how creatively the tricks are linked together. "Switching" moves (performing more than one trick during a grind) will also add to a skater's score as will performing "lip tricks" – tricks on the coping of a ramp (see page 22). "Unnatural" also earns extra points – a skater raises his or her hand to indicate to the judges that a move will be performed in this way.

STYLING IT

It is important to "style" your moves. This means that your whole body must look good when you perform a grind. You must look well balanced and in control, and, by varying your body position, you can earn more points for style in competitions.

23

Roller hockey

Roller hockey is increasing in popularity. It has all the thrill and excitement of ice hockey, on which it is based, but it is played on the streets, in school gymnasiums, and in recreation centers – almost anywhere it can be played safely.

Once you are confident with your basic in-line moves and stops, join in an informal game of in-line hockey, often called pick-up hockey. It's a quick and fun way to learn how to control your skates and speed.

The goalie (above) *wears more protection than the other players!*

TEAMS

Roller hockey is a team sport *(right)*. Most forms of the game are played with four outfield players (two attackers and two defenders) and a goalie. The game allows an individual to demonstrate his or her skills, but the success of a team depends upon the ability of the players to work well together.

You can play hockey on quads or in-line skates.

HOCKEY GEAR

Your skates need to be as tough and as light as possible. You can buy specialized skates (right) *or you can adapt regular skates by fitting the appropriate wheels and rockering them* (see page 8). *Wear the full protective gear and a hockey helmet, ideally with a full-face shield* (above left).

THE BASIC GAME

Roller hockey is played with a long stick *(far right)* made from wood or metal, and a weighted puck, or ball. The aim of the game is to put the puck into the net as many times as possible. Some forms of hockey allow physical contact; others do not. Roller hockey can be played in venues of all sizes.

25

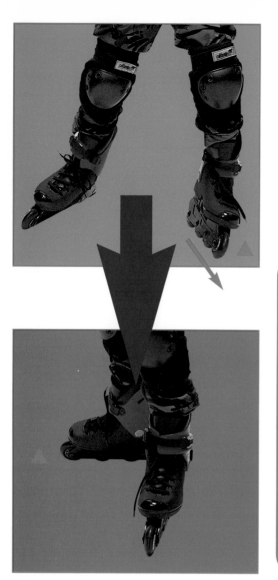

WHAT A DRAG!

In the drag stop, or T-stop, the friction from your trailing wheels slows you down. Support your weight on your front skate. This skate points in the direction in which you are moving (top left). Lower your trailing skate gently to the ground so that the wheels are at a 90° angle to the direction in which you are traveling. Apply downward pressure with your trailing skate (below left).

Use your arms and your waist to prevent you from spinning. If you practice this too fast, you will spin out of control.

HELP!

In-liners face some common problems that are easily corrected if you follow some basic principles:
* Start at a very slow speed. Build up your speed gradually. Do not try to perform any stops at a fast speed until you can perform them well from a slow skating speed.
* Use the ready position *(see pages 12-13)* to help keep your balance as you stop. Keep your knees bent. Don't be tempted to lean backward with straight legs *(right)*.
* Never go faster than the speed at which you know you can safely stop.

SPIN STOP

Practice this stop at VERY slow speeds to start with.

Take your weight onto your leading foot ☐1. If you are turning to the left this will be your right foot. If you are turning to the right this will be your left foot. Lift the back wheel of your trailing skate, keeping the front wheel on the ground ☐2.

Turn this skate to a right angle to your leading skate. Lower it to the ground ☐3. As you do so your body will turn in the direction of the trailing skate ☐4. The spinning action will bring you to a halt ☐5. To control the movement, flex your ankles and legs. Make sure that you are leaning forward and not backward.

POWER SLIDE

For this variation of an impressive but difficult move, bend both your knees 1. *Raise the heel of your right skate and turn it to face outward. Move your weight onto this trailing foot (in this example, right foot)* 2.

Bending low, swing the left skate out in a large arc. Bring the right heel to the ground 3. *Bring your left skate to the ground at a right angle. Your left leg is straight; your right knee is bent* 4 . *Keep your body low.*

Learning to stop!

You already know the heel-brake stop *(see page 15),* but there are several other ways to stop. Practice as many as possible because each one will be useful in different situations. If you are an "aggressive" or speed skater, or if you play roller hockey, you will not often use the heel-brake stop, so it is particularly important for you to learn other forms of stopping.

HOCKEY STOP

This is an advanced stop often used for skating on indoor surfaces. Only advanced-level skaters should attempt this stop (right). Make sure that you are familiar with the surface on which you are skating – otherwise you will fall. The body quickly twists so that both skates turn through a 90° angle. The friction of all eight wheels brings you to a stop.

Moving onto grass from pavement (left) is a quick and easy way to stop.

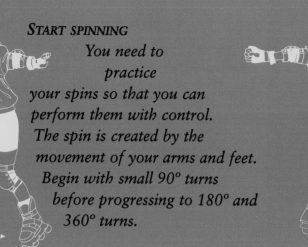

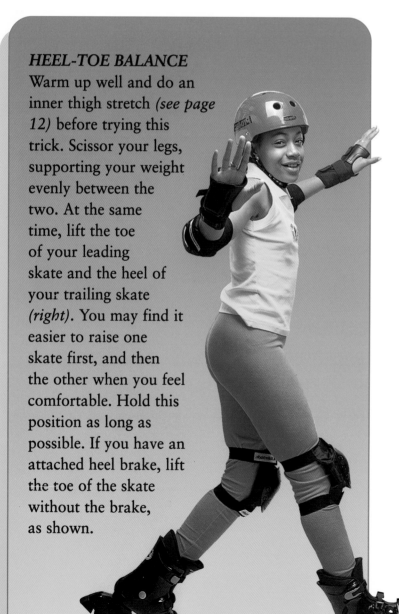

START SPINNING
You need to practice your spins so that you can perform them with control. The spin is created by the movement of your arms and feet. Begin with small 90° turns before progressing to 180° and 360° turns.

Stand with your skates approximately shoulder width apart. Begin with a 90° turn to the left. Swing your arms to your left; at the same time rise onto the toe of your left skate. Lift the heel of your right skate. Drop it back down when you have completed your 90° turn.

HEEL-TOE BALANCE

Warm up well and do an inner thigh stretch *(see page 12)* before trying this trick. Scissor your legs, supporting your weight evenly between the two. At the same time, lift the toe of your leading skate and the heel of your trailing skate *(right)*. You may find it easier to raise one skate first, and then the other when you feel comfortable. Hold this position as long as possible. If you have an attached heel brake, lift the toe of the skate without the brake, as shown.

Step 1: Lean to the left, taking all your weight onto your left foot.

1

CROSS-OVER TURNS

These turns look great and they allow you to take a corner without losing any speed. You can actually accelerate using this turn. To perform a cross-over turn, you need to develop confidence supporting all your weight on your inside skate while leaning into the turn. In the sequence *(above and opposite)* the skater is turning to the left. The position of her weight is indicated by the blue triangle. First practice this with small cross-over steps. As you gain confidence you can increase their range.

28

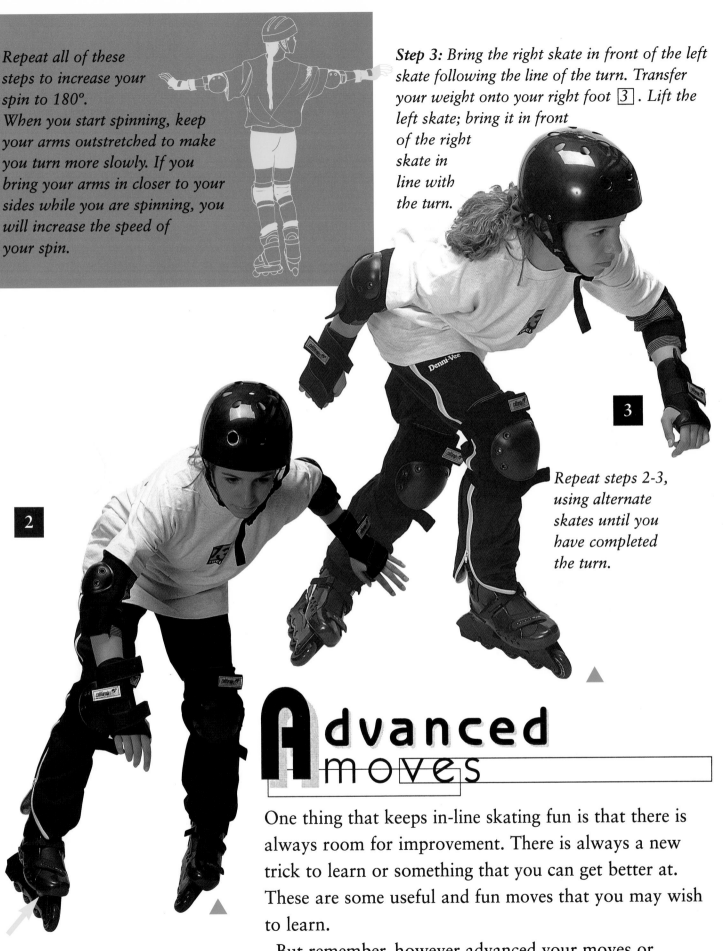

Repeat all of these steps to increase your spin to 180°.
When you start spinning, keep your arms outstretched to make you turn more slowly. If you bring your arms in closer to your sides while you are spinning, you will increase the speed of your spin.

Step 3: Bring the right skate in front of the left skate following the line of the turn. Transfer your weight onto your right foot 3 . Lift the left skate; bring it in front of the right skate in line with the turn.

Repeat steps 2-3, using alternate skates until you have completed the turn.

Advanced moves

One thing that keeps in-line skating fun is that there is always room for improvement. There is always a new trick to learn or something that you can get better at. These are some useful and fun moves that you may wish to learn.

But remember, however advanced your moves or tricks, pad up well. It doesn't look, or feel, very good if you hurt yourself.

Step 2: Lift your right skate off the ground, keeping your weight on your left skate.

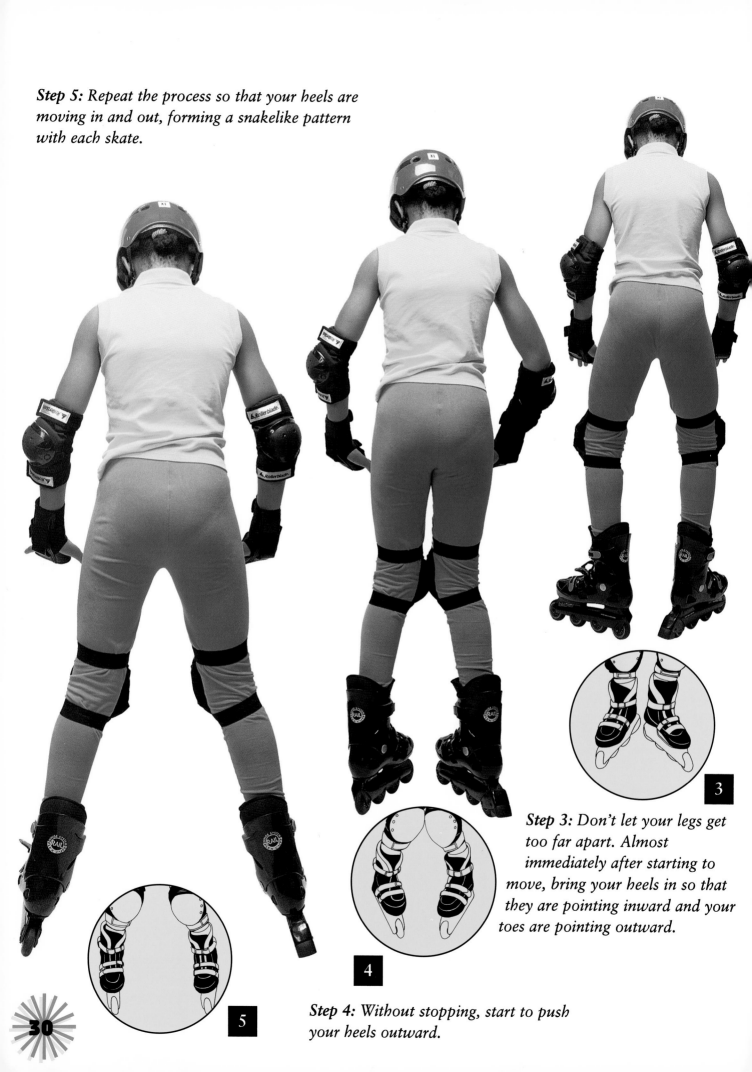

Step 5: *Repeat the process so that your heels are moving in and out, forming a snakelike pattern with each skate.*

3

Step 3: Don't let your legs get too far apart. Almost immediately after starting to move, bring your heels in so that they are pointing inward and your toes are pointing outward.

4

5

Step 4: Without stopping, start to push your heels outward.

When an "aggressive" skater, such as Brian Smith from Venice, California *(below)*, makes it to the top, he or she can become a professional skater. He or she may be approached by an in-line skate company who will sponsor, or pay, the skater. In return, the skater promotes the company and its products. You can see skaters such as Brian doing the latest moves at "aggressive" events and shows.

Step 1: *Start with the front of your skates pointing inward and your heels outward. Keep your knees bent and all your wheels in contact with the ground.*

Step 2: *Gently push outward using pressure from the front, or toe, part of your skate.*

ON ONE LEG

Improve your skating the quick way! Practicing on one skate will help you with a lot of the advanced moves and stops many of which, such as the power slide *(see page 27)*, that often require you to support all of your weight on one skate. Gradually build up the distance you can skate on one leg. Try it on the other leg, too! After a while, try a snake pattern on one leg *(right)*.

Skating backward

Everybody wants to skate backward. It looks great – and it's fun to do. The backward swizzle is the best way to learn how to skate backward. It is also known as the "snake pattern" or the "hour-glass" because of the pattern made by the path of your skates.

First practice your steps without moving at speed. If you feel unsure to begin with, give yourself a gentle push from a wall. When you actually start to move, look over your shoulder to check that it is safe for you to start skating.

Before you actually take off, think about your landing – it is very important not to fall backward on landing. You need to land with your legs apart and slightly scissored, and your weight slightly forward (left).

Start your jumps from a stationary position. To begin with, aim low rather than high. Use your arms to provide the momentum to lift you off the ground. Once you feel confident about your landing technique, try taking off while moving slowly.

STAIR JUMPING

After jumping on flat surfaces, in-line skaters often progress to getting more air by launching off stairs. But remember, start on a drop of only one or two steps and gradually build up the number of steps you can jump. When you are at an advanced level, try landing "fakie" (backward) after turning through 180° in the air.

Styling the air

If you thought that skating only involved stroking and gliding on flat ground, think again! "Aggressive" skaters, and sometimes "rec" skaters, enjoy the thrill of using the momentum, or force, gained from rolling on skates to launch themselves into the air. Jumping, more often known as "airing," has become a major part of "aggressive" skating with styled airs bringing high scores in competition. It is spectacular, and the added difficulty of landing big airs brings lots of thrills. Before attempting even the smallest jumps, make sure you are wearing adequate padding and your helmet.

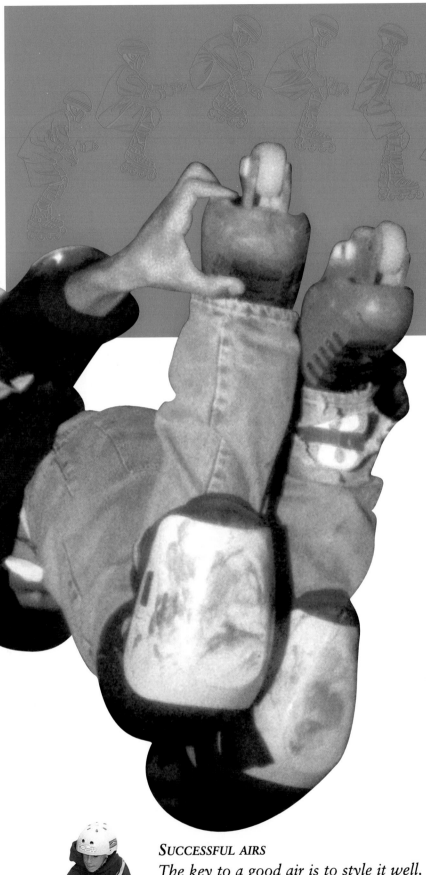

FLAT OR RAMP?

On flat ground the only lift you get is from your legs, so you don't get nearly as much air (left) as you do with ramps. A ramp is a launchpad that gives your airs extra height. Once you're confident, try jumping over small obstacles to add a new challenge to your skating.

LANDING TECHNIQUE

Landing is the most crucial part of airing. Whatever you do in the air should bring you back or put you into position for a safe, solid landing. The most stable way to land is with your legs scissored and your weight forward. Have your front leg bent in front of you and your trailing leg bent so that you can just drop onto your knee pad if necessary. This method helps to keep you close to the ground, and reduces the possibility of you falling backward.

SUCCESSFUL AIRS

The key to a good air is to style it well. This means that you must make your move look controlled, easy, and compact (above and left). A smaller air with a neat position is much better than a high air with arms and legs flailing. Remember, don't just air it... style it!

OFF-ROAD IN-LINE

Off-road skating is a new and popular development in in-line skating. An extra long aluminum frame with large wheels at either end *(below and right)* allows skaters to travel over rough and rocky ground. Off-roaders will find a stretch of ground over which they can roll on their skates, and aim for some big airs.

CROSS TRAINING
In-line skating is an excellent, fun way to improve your training program (left), *whatever sport you are involved in. It supplies all the exercise benefits of jogging without placing pressure on your joints. As well as being fun, skating can also be serious physical exercise.*

Other styles

In-line skating is an incredibly diverse sport, ranging from speed racing *(far left)* to "aggressive" skating *(right)*. People are always inventing new ways to enjoy it. Games such as catch, tennis, basketball, and even football take on a new twist when you play them on wheels! In the future you may see new developments in the sport from off-road racing to long-jump championships.

"Aggressive" skaters are equipped and ready to go (below).

FREESTYLE
No limits, no rules, and any place – as long as it is safe; freestyle skating is filled with exciting moves and sequences that are as much fun to watch as they are to perform. Freestyle is often performed with music and has a dance feel to it.

ENJOY IT!
The key to skating success is enjoyment! Don't worry if you are a beginner practicing your "duck" steps and another skater goes whizzing by. Everyone has to start at the beginning! With practice you will make progress. Whatever your level, the most important factor must be safety for you and those around you.

If you enjoy team sports, why not join a club or a team? And if you can't find one, start your own! It's a great way to meet new friends and skating buddies. Skate clubs exist for everyone from "rec" skaters to fitness fanatics and competition skaters.

IN-LINE HISTORY

Did you know that in-line skates are over 100 years old? Their predecessor, the roller skate, or quad, was developed in the 1700s is still used today. In the 1800s, iron in-line skates were developed.

Up until the 1970s a few design improvements were made. (below).

However, in-line skates only really took off when Scott Olson, an ice-hockey player, developed a pair of skates on which he could train all year round. Modern in-liners were made – and the rest is history!

For years, people of all ages have enjoyed skating on quads.

Skate care for safety

Your in-line skates are specialized items of sporting equipment. If you want to make the most of them, you will need to maintain and care for them properly. This means checking them for wear and tear and cleaning them regularly.

By looking after your skates they will last longer and perform better. They will also keep you safe.

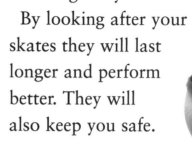

PUT YOUR BRAKES ON!
Brakes wear down from constant use. Make sure that you replace them before they reach the end of the rubber. If you have screws attaching your heel brake to the chassis, be sure that they are tight so that the brake is secure and does not vibrate.

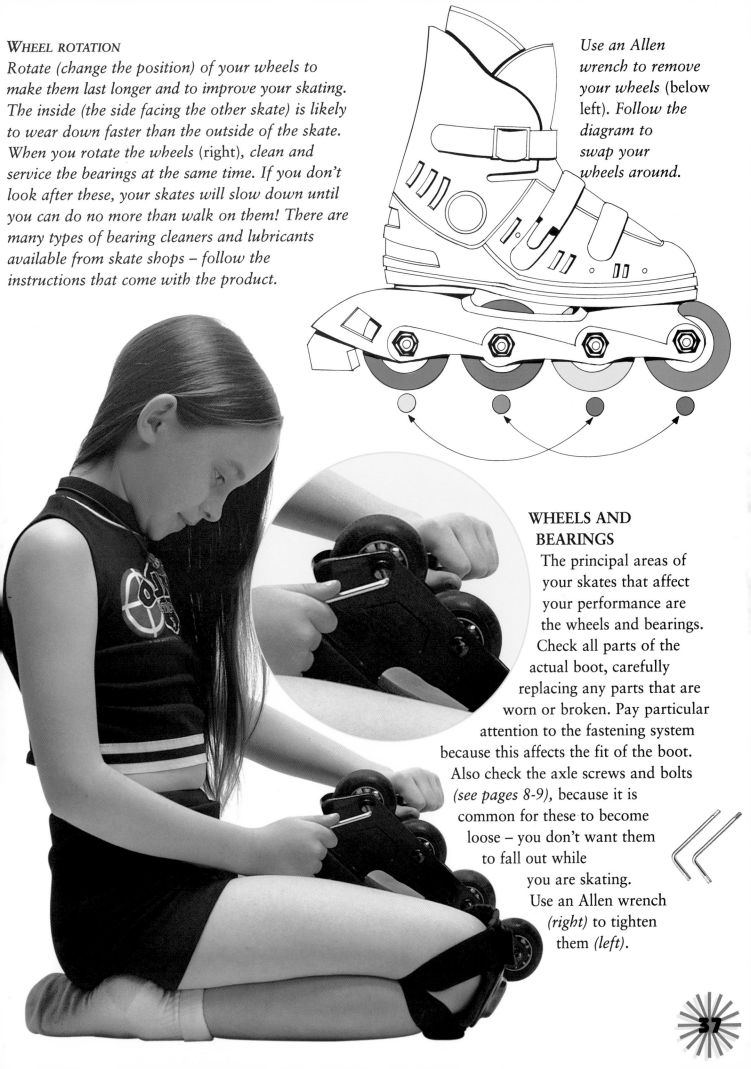

WHEEL ROTATION

Rotate (change the position) of your wheels to make them last longer and to improve your skating. The inside (the side facing the other skate) is likely to wear down faster than the outside of the skate. When you rotate the wheels (right), *clean and service the bearings at the same time. If you don't look after these, your skates will slow down until you can do no more than walk on them! There are many types of bearing cleaners and lubricants available from skate shops – follow the instructions that come with the product.*

Use an Allen wrench to remove your wheels (below left). Follow the diagram to swap your wheels around.

WHEELS AND BEARINGS

The principal areas of your skates that affect your performance are the wheels and bearings. Check all parts of the actual boot, carefully replacing any parts that are worn or broken. Pay particular attention to the fastening system because this affects the fit of the boot. Also check the axle screws and bolts *(see pages 8-9),* because it is common for these to become loose – you don't want them to fall out while you are skating. Use an Allen wrench *(right)* to tighten them *(left).*

Streetwise and safe

Apart from wearing all of your pads, including your helmet, every time you skate, you should also be very careful where you skate – especially when you are learning. Find a place which is smooth and level – stay away from slopes and hills. It should also be well away from traffic and pedestrians. Public parks where skating is allowed and cycle paths are good places to start. Stay away from pavements near roads and streets until you are able to stop and control your speed.

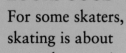

STAIRS AND CURBS
When learning, slow down before stepping up or down curbs or stairs (right). *Lean forward over the curb before stepping up. Practicing skating on one foot will help you with curbs, as you need to support all your weight on one skate. If you are unsure, remove both your skates to go up and down stairs.*

LOOKS GOOD
For some skaters, skating is about more than a pair of skates. It's about a comb in the back pocket, a baseball cap, the right T-shirt, a skater's bag, a spare wheel hanging on a chain... *(left).* But for other skaters, it's just the skating that matters!

OFF THE GRAVEL!
When you are learning, every crack, bit of grit, twig, or stone can cause your wheels to lock and make you fall. If you are on such a surface (above), *make yourself more stable by scissoring your legs.*

HILLS
Only attempt hills (right) *when you have perfected your speed control and stopping skills. If you are a beginner, take off your skates and walk – it's much safer!*

Skate Speak

"Aggressive" skating
Skating that uses props such as ramps and rails. It is also called extreme or stunt skating.

Airs
Jumps or tricks in which you leave the ground.

Allen wrench
A tool which is used to remove the wheels from skates. An Allen key can also be used to tighten up the screws and bolts on skates.

Bearing
A round object which helps a wheel to spin.

Chassis
The bottom part of an in-line skate that holds the wheels.

Coping
The point on a ramp where the "vert" meets the deck.

Deck
The platform area of a ramp.

"Duck" walk
The small practice steps taken by a beginner.

Fakie
To land or to skate backward.

Freestyle
A form of recreational skating with tricks. It is often performed to music.

Gliding
The free rolling of skates.

Grind Plates
Plates that are attached to skates to perform grinds.

Grinds
Sliding with in-line skates on curbs, handrails, and ledges.

Half pipe
A ramp that looks similar to a large pipe cut in half.

Off-road skating
Skating on rocky terrain.

Pads
Essential protective covering for elbows and knees. It can also refer to wrist guards.

Quads
Roller skates with four wheels arranged in a rectangle.

Quarter pipe
A ramp that resembles the shape of a pipe cut into a quarter.

Ramps
Launches for tricks and jumps. They include half pipes, quarter pipes, and "verts."

Recreational skating
In-line skating for fun.

Roller hockey
Hockey on in-line skates.

Scissoring
The position in which one leg is placed in front of the other leg.

Sessioning
Spending time skating on particular ramps or rails.

Spacers
A spacer is a piece of plastic or metal which holds the bearings at a fixed distance from each other.

Speed skating
In-line skating for speed.

Striding
The combination of stroking and gliding.

Stroking
The push and thrust from the trailing leg to power movement.

Swizzle
A skating movement in which your wheels stay in contact with the ground.

Thrust
The pushing action of the trailing skate to create forward movement.

Tweaking
Exaggerating a trick or move.

Vert
The part of a ramp that is vertical.

Index

Photo Credits: *Abbreviations: t-top, m-middle, b-bottom, r-right, l-left, c-center*

Front cover, 2, 3, 8-9 all, 10-11 all, 12-13 all, 14-15 all, 16m, 26-27 all, 28-29 all, 30 all, 31l, 32b, 34bl, 36mr, 37-38 all – Roger Vlitos; 1 & 18ml – Andy Critchlow/Inline Skatermag; 4-5, 33bl, 35r & m – Frank Spooner Pictures; 6l, 7b, 23tr both, 23mrb & br all, 25m & 35b – Archie King/Skaters Paradise; 6r, 6-7, 17t, 25t & 34r – Sandy Chalmers/Inline Skatermag; 7t – Graham Burkitt/Inline Skatermag; 16t – Rob Tysall; 17m & b, 18t, mr & b, 19 all, 20-22 all, 23mc, & mrt; 31tc & 32-33 – Paul Rickelton; 23tl – Inline Skatermag; 23bl & 34tl – Brian Wood/Inline Skatermag; 24b – Aldie Chalmers/Inline Skatermag; 36t & ml – Hulton Getty Collection.

The publishers would like to thank Archie and Mathew King and everyone at Skaters Paradise for their help and cooperation in the preparation of this book.